Mike Eccles

PEARS
DUOLOGUES

★ ✦

HEATHER STEPHENS

*with new adaptations
of part scenes from
the classic play
Peace by
Aristophanes
&
the Victorian novel
Oliver Twist by
Dickens*

*Dramatic Lines**

DRAMATIC LINES, TWICKENHAM, ENGLAND
text copyright © Heather Stephens

This book is intended to provide performance material for speech and drama festivals, examinations workshops or for use in schools and colleges. No permission is required for amateur performance.

Application for performance by professional companies should be made to:

Dramatic Lines PO Box 201
Twickenham TW2 5RQ
England

A CIP record for this book is available from the British Library

ISBN 0 9522224 6 9

Pears first published 1997 by
Dramatic Lines Twickenham England
All rights reserved

Printed by The Basingstoke Press (75) Ltd
Hampshire England

ACKNOWLEDGMENTS

My very grateful thanks to:

Shaun McKenna
Principal of Examinations LAMDA
and
Peter Egan
the distinguished
Shakespearian
film and television actor
and theatrical director

for their invaluable advice
and encouragement

CONTENTS

OLIVER TWIST

OLIVER AND HIS NEGLECTED SCRUFFY COMPANIONS SUFFER THE
EFFECTS OF SLOW STARVATION IN THE WORKHOUSE FOR MONTHS
BEFORE OLIVER IS CHOSEN TO WALK UP AND DEMAND MORE
GRUEL ONE SUPPERTIME: EARLY THE FOLLOWING MORNING FRIZ
AND SPIKE ARE PUT TO WORK UNRAVELLING LENGTHS OF OLD
ROPE OUTSIDE IN THE COLD INADEQUATELY DRESSED IN RAGGED
CLOTHING AND ILL-FITTING BOOTS.

FRIZ AND SPIKE ARE SEATED ON WOODEN CRATES/PACKING CASES
CENTRE STAGE. A LARGE PILE OF OLD ROPE LIES TO ONE SIDE
WITHIN ARM'S LENGTH WITH A SMALL HEAP OF UNRAVELLED
FIBROUS STRANDS CLOSEBY. THEY WORK MECHANICALLY IN
THOUGHTFUL SILENCE.

> FRIZ: A DOMINANT PERSONALITY, LIVELY ALL-KNOWING SURVIVOR
> SPIKE: WITH TUBERCULAR COUGH & HABIT OF WIPING NOSE ON SLEEVE
> FEELS THE COLD TERRIBLY

FRIZ: (Pausing)
You gotta hand it to'im.
'E came up with the goods.

SPIKE STOPS WORK AND YAWNS AND SCRATCHES

SPIKE: An' look where it got 'im.
I wouldn'tve liked to've bin the one!

FRIZ DROPS A HANDFUL OF STRANDS ON THE HEAP

FRIZ: But if you'dve drawn the short straw
you'dve **had** to've bin the one to go up.
Wouldn't you, Spike?
That's what was agreed.

SPIKE: (Hastily) Oh! Yeah.

FRIZ: We held a meeting, remember?

SPIKE: Course I do!
On account've the one with the wild hungry look
about-the-eyes.

FRIZ: **Lofty!**

SPIKE: ..... on account've Lofty
'hinting' that he was likely to eat the sickly young'n
who slept next to 'im

1

unless 'e was giv'n another bowl've gruel a day.

FRIZ SUCKS ON NUCKLES ENTHUSIASTICALLY

FRIZ: 'E might well've done, too.
'E looked capable.
(Pause)
Couldn't exacly blame Lofty though, could you?
Three titchey bowls of thin gruel a day,
an onion twice a week and half-a-roll on Sundays.
What do you expect?
'E were **desperate** with 'unger!

SPIKE: (Hastily) We was all desperate!
We was all starving hungry.

FRIZ: So **'someone'** had to walk up and ask.
Didn't they?

SPIKE NODS HASTILY

SPIKE: An'it fell to Oliver Twist!

FRIZ TOUSSLES SPIKE'S HAIR AFFECTIONATELY

FRIZ: (Respectfully) Shan't forget what young Oliver Twist did
in a hurry, neither.
(Shifting closer to Spike)
Mind you.... after the gruel was served out
and we was sat in our places
I began to 'ave doubts, I'd be the first to admit.

FRIZ SELECTS A SHORT PIECE OF ROPE

SPIKE: Didn't you think 'E'd go through wiv it, then?

SPIKE SCRATCHES HEAD

FRIZ: But just as soon as the gruel'd disappeared
an' every bowl in the hall empty.
I **knew** it were on!
Then all that whispering started up.
Wiv everyone lookin'ard at Oliver:
(Winking in exaggerated manner)
then staring down the end of the hall at the copper.
(Laughing and smiling)
Cor! What a sight!

2

Sir, beside the copper with the cook's apron stretched
around 'is paunch an' a ladle in 'is 'and
not 'aving a clue about nothink!
An' every last one of us egging Oliver on.
(Nudging Spike) Every way you 'could think of.

FRIZ WALKS FOWARD WITH AN IMAGINARY BOWL.

FRIZ: (Addressing the audience)
'Please, sir, I want some more.'

SPIKE VIEWS FRIZ'S BACK WITH ADMIRATION
AND RISES SLOWLY TO FEET

SPIKE: An' Sir turns chalk-white.
(Pause)
Stares dumbfounded ... at Oliver.
(Mimicking the action)
Clings onto the kettle;
knocked senseless.

FRIZ: Could've heard a pin drop.

SPIKE: (Imitating the master's faint voice) 'What!'

FRIZ: (Addressing the audience) 'Please sir, I want some more.'

SPIKE: Sir .....
..... recovers 'is senses.
An' swipes at Oliver's head wiv the ladle .....

FRIZ DUCKS AND DIVES IN FRONT AS
SPIKE SIMULTANEOUSLY SWIPES AT THE AIR

SPIKE: ..... An' Oliver's frogmarched off; locked up.

FRIZ RUMMAGES IN THE PILE OF ROPE

FRIZ: (Quietly) You've gotta take yer hat off to Oliver .....

FRIZ AND SPIKE TAKE UP ORIGIONAL POSITIONS ON
THE CRATES AND ATTEMPT TO WARM HANDS AND
FEET BEFORE COMMENCING WORK

FRIZ: But that's the last any've us will ever see of 'im, I'd say. Spike.
The very last.

FRIZ AND SPIKE LAPSE INTO SILENCE

3

THE ZIT

STACY AND LUDO ARE DESPERATELY FASHION CONSCIOUS BEST FRIENDS. LUDO IS SKIMMING A TEEN MAGAZINE WHILST WAITING FOR STACY TO COMPLETE THE FINAL TOUCHES TO MAKEUP AND NEWLY STYLED HAIR BEFORE THEY HIT THE TOWN.

TWO ARMCHAIRS, LUDO IS SITTING ON A RUG LEANING AGAINST ONE OF THE ARMCHAIRS, STACY PARADES IN 'THE NEW OUTFIT'.

LUDO:	(Looking up) Cool gear babe.
	STACY SMILES, PERCHES ON A CHAIRARM AND OPENS UP AN OVERSIZE MAKEUP BAG
LUDO:	(Reading aloud) 'Makeover Magic!' ...... Before and after piccies. (Pulling a face) Joke! (Holding up the magazine for Stacy to see)
STACY:	Sad!
	STACY MINUTELY EXAMINES INDIVIDUAL SKIN PORES IN A MIRROR
LUDO:	(Flicking through and stopping at beauty/fashion spread) Dreamy! Drool, drool! (Flicking and stopping) **Wild!** (Licking finger, thumbing through pages) Dodgy! (Turning a page) Wanna give this month's quiz a shot, Stace?
	STACY CONCENTRATES HARD ON TRIVIAL ADJUSTMENTS TO MAKEUP
STACY:	Nah!
LUDO:	Stace, hear this: you'll crack up! 'Do you treat blokes like aliens?'
STACY:	(Pausing to think) Is that for real?
LUDO:	'Are you convinced males are from planet Zog?'
STACY:	(Cutting in) Trashy stuff or what?
LUDO:	(Cutting in) 'Are you galactically guy-wise?'

STACY:	Sad!
LUDO:	(Consulting watch) Are you nearly done, Stace? Get a move on, wild child. Ttt ... (Pause) ... ttt. Ttt! Stace.

STACY SHOOTS LUDO A WARNING LOOK

LUDO:	(Quickly) Stace, you look gorge. (Pause) (Sighing loudly) No problem. I'll take root; grow into a couch potato by the time you've glammed up, that's all! (Pause) (Snappily) Nothing to worry your head about, Stace! But today would be nice!
STACY:	Stop rattling your cage.
LUDO:	Chill out, mate!
STACY:	(Standing) What's the hurry: I'm on my way.
LUDO:	Brill. (Jumping up and holding magazine under Ludo's nose) 'Snogging a saddo'
STACY:	Yeuuch!
LUDO:	(Throwing down the magazine) Like you do!
STACY:	Nah!
LUDO:	**Stace!** (Pointing at Stacy's nose)
STACY:	(Cutting in anxiously) What?
LUDO:	Give us that mirror. (Holding up the mirror for Stacy to look)
STACY:	(Shrieking) **Vesuvius!**
LUDO:	(Awestruck) Who knew a zit could errupt like that?
STACY:	**I'm gutted!**

LUDO:	Talk about blow your mind! Blew up faster than popcorn.
STACY: **LUDO:**	That's right, give me grief ..... (Cutting in) Crikey! So I'm to blame? (Uncomfortable Silence) Stace........... it hardly notices.
STACY:	Ludo! I don't give a flying fig what you think. I'd rather be seen dead than go out on a date with my nose lurking behind the megga dayglo zit of all time!

STACY DIVES FOR THE NEAREST ARMCHAIR,
BURIES AND LUDO RETRIEVES THE MAGAZINE

LUDO:	Stace! (Pause) Stace! (Stace reluctantly lifts head) Take your mind off've it.

STACE HESITATES, SNATCHES THE MAGAZINE
WITHOUT A WORD AND TURNS A PAGE OR TWO

STACE:	(Reading aloud) '..... lotion to help keep pores free of zit-friendly gunge!' (Infuriated) **Joke!**
LUDO:	No need to throw a wobbly!
STACY:	(Brandishing magazine) **Joke?**
LUDO:	Nah! Didn't give it for that reason. No need to go on and on, Stace. The zit's no bigger than a pinhead!
STACY: **LUDO:**	(Cutting in) .....Wish I'd never clapped eyes on you! Go back to planet Zog where you belong! (Cutting in) You're off the wall .....
STACY: **LUDO:**	Low-life! (Cutting in) Best mate from hell!

STACY THROWS MAGAZINE AT LUDO AND RUNS

EXIT STACY.

STACY:	(Horrified) Crikey! Intergalactic war over a zit.

NEVER THE BRIDESMAID

ROSIE IS REVELLING IN THE DESCRIPTION OF A RECENT WEDDING AT WHICH SHE WAS A BRIDESMAID FOR THE THIRD TIME. SHE HAS DRESSED UP IN THE BRIDESMAID'S DRESS TO IMPRESS JESSICA (WEARING JEANS AND TEE SHIRT), HER ENVIOUS BEST FRIEND, WHO YEARNS TO BE A BRIDESMAID.

ROSIE:	I carried ...(Walking sedately) ... a basket of beautiful beautiful roses.
	JESSICA LOOKS ON LONGINGLY
JESSICA:	Oh! Rosie.
ROSIE:	And I wore a circle of real flowers around my head on the day; like an angel's halo.
JESSICA:	I've **always** longed to wear flowers in my hair, Rosie.
ROSIE:	Everyone thought that the flowers were just **'me'**. (Pause) Even the Bride said I looked as pretty as a picture.
JESSICA: **ROSIE:**	Mummy said ..... (Cutting in) I've been a bridesmaid three times already. So I know exactly what to do: I'm professional. (Curtsying) I wore pretty pretty almond pink wild silk the first time, white satin with lacy petticoats the next. (Twirling around) And this, last Saturday.
JESSICA: **ROSIE:**	Mummy said ..... (Cutting in) Jessica. You've **never ever** been chosen to be a bridesmaid, have you?
JESSICA:	No! Not once.
ROSIE:	Poor, poor Jessica. I feel **ever-so-sorry** for you, Really I do.
JESSICA:	Mummy said the only reason that I hadn't was because .....

ROSIE:	(Cutting in) Oh! Silly me! I haven't shown you my shoes yet. I almost forgot: how could I? (Lifting skirt) Look! Jessica. Cost-a-fortune. (Pointing toes daintily) But perfect with the dress.
JESSICA:	Mummy said that the only reason that you're chosen to be a bridesmaid is .....
ROSIE:	(Cutting in) You're jealous! **Green** with envy. I've spent all this time telling you about the wedding because I thought you were interested because you're supposed to be my friend. It's hardly **my** fault that you've never ever been chosen. Is it?

ROSIE SWEEPS OFF

EXIT ROSIE.

JESSICA:	(Shouting) Rosie! Mummy said the reason you're so popular as a bridesmaid is because your Mother promises to write a massive cheque as a wedding present. (Pause) My Mummy calls it bribery. And says its contemptible. (To herself) And gave **me** a lecture when I asked her to do the same for me. Just once: just the once: that's all I wanted. It's not fair. (Stamping feet in temper)

BLONDIE

Sydney 13 January 1957, a party of 60 unwilling participants in the British government child migration scheme arrived on the Asturias cruise ship from England. Two sisters were sent directly to a Western Australia Institution. The younger one, Blondie cried bitterly for days before packing her bag and running off down the drive in her nightdress. The nuns in charge followed and dragged her back. All the institution children were woken, lined up in the yard and forced to watch her punishment.

BLONDIE'S OLDER SISTER: VERY PROTECTIVE TOWARDS HER 5 YEAR OLD SISTER, SHOCKED AND TRAUMATISED BY OVERNIGHT EVENTS AT THE INSTITUTION WHICH COMPARES SO UNFAVOURABLY WITH THEIR FORMER CHILDREN'S HOME IN ENGLAND. **INSTITUTION CHILD:** ALSO AFFECTED BY THE INCIDENT BUT TOUGHENED BY INSTITUTION LIFE WHILST RETAINING A HEALTHY NATURAL CURIOUSITY AND KINDLY DISPOSITION TOWARDS NEW GIRLS.

THE BAREFOOT GIRLS ARE DRESSED IN UTILITY NIGHTDRESSES. BLONDIE'S SISTER FACES THE AUDIENCE AND STANDS ABSOLUTELY STILL WITHOUT DISPLAYING EMOTION. THE INSTITUTION CHILD WALKS UP SLOWLY BEHIND HER, HESITATES A WHILE BEFORE FINALLY SPEAKING FROM BEHIND.

CHILD:	You're the blonde girl's big sister, aren't you?
	SISTER NODS AND GRUNTS WITHOUT TURNING
CHILD:	.....How is she?
SISTER:	(Shrugging) Don't know. (Pause) She's with Reverend Mother.
CHILD:	(Hesitantly) She shouldn'tve run away.
	SISTER SWINGS AROUND, THE CHILD RETREATS
SISTER:	(Defensively) Blondie's only five .... Five's to young to understand consequences.
	SISTER WALKS OFF CHILD MOVES CLOSE TO TOUCH HER ARM
CHILD:	(Gently) They made an example of her to stop anyone else trying. (Pause) That's why the punishment was ..... heartless.

SISTER:	Punishment for what? Feeling appallingly homesick and unhappy? For being desperate to escape from the Institution? (Pause) Was she **really** punished for packing her bag and running off into the bush after dark barefoot in a nightie? ..... or was she punished for having beautiful long blonde curls and a pretty face?
CHILD:	Word's out that your sister **infuriated** the nuns. That she ran like the wind down the drive chased by nuns running flat out holding up their skirts. And that they finally cornered her outside the gates.
SISTER:	They swooped down ...... dragged her back screaming by the hair.
CHILD:	(Awkwardly) We've never been woken in the middle of the night and lined up in the yard before: no one else has ever dared to run away.
SISTER:	And will Blondie's humiliation insure that she's the last, I wonder?
CHILD:	(Hastily) We didn't want to watch .....
SISTER:	(Sighing) I can't get the pictures out of my mind .....

CHILD SQUIRMS UNCOMFORTABLY UNDER HER GAZE

CHILD:	(Quietly to herself) .....didn't want to watch.
SISTER:	.... two nuns forcefully restraining a defiant small child. Nuns, eyes blazing with religious fervour patrolling our lines, poking torches in our faces, blinding us with torchlight.
CHILD:	They **forced** us all to watch.
SISTER:	I was hauled out of line. Pushed foward to stand by myself in front of my little sister.
SISTER:	(Pause) I was struck dumb, rooted to the spot.
CHILD:	There was nothing any of us could do.

SISTER: My little sister struggled and screamed,
              cried out for help
              but **we** all stood by
              did **nothing**
              even after the third nun began to hack at her hair with garden
              shears.

CHILD: (Quietly) It was a futile struggle;
              her defiance made matters worse.

SISTER: **How dare you say that?**
              She was terrified, that's why she fought to free herself.
              Everyone ignored her cries for help:
              ignored her screams.
              (Pause)
              The nuns were merciless.
              No pity .... no forgiveness.
              (Long pause)
              No love .....
              Poor Blondie.
              Did you realise that there was only
              (holding up thumb and finger)
              that much spikey hair left
              when **The Creature** finally put down the shears?

              SISTER TURNS HER FACE AWAY

CHILD: ..... I'm so so sorry!
              But there was **nothing** we could do.

SISTER: She was trembling uncontrollably,
              breathing heavily, sobbing without making a sound.

              CHILD TURNS AWAY

SISTER: Strands of long platinum hair
              lay heaped in the dust at her feet
              but Blondie's eyes were fixed on a far-distant star
              and her jaw was set firm.

              CHILD TURNS BACK SLOWLY AND RELUCTANTLY
              SISTER CLAPS HANDS OVER HER EARS

SISTER: (Shouting) **'God wants her punished more than that!'**
              And **The Creature** produced a pair of secateurs from thin air.
              (Pause)
              She .....
              cut cut cut cut ...

11

CHILD BOWS HER HEAD

CHILD: ...... I ..

SISTER: **The Creature** cut brutally.
Didn't stop ......
..... until the hair was completely gone.
(Pause)
Blondie's scalp was bloody with cuts.
(Long Pause)
I watched a droplet of blood trickle down her tear-stained face
and I didn't say a word.
Didn't move foward to hold her, to comfort her.
(Pause)
I..... failed her.

CHILD AND SISTER STAND IN AWKWARD SILENCE

THE OUTBACK INSTITUTION

Unpublicised twentieth century British government child migration schemes existed for the long term purpose of populating bleak areas of the Empire and providing an unpaid agricultural and domestic child labour force whilst representing a hypothetical 'financial saving' for British economy statistics. One hundred and fifty thousand unaccompanied boys and girls had been transported from British children's homes to British Commonwealth institutions by 1967. Child migrants, as young as four, were stripped of identity and birthdate and falsely led to believe that their parents were dead; and numerous suffered untold physical and emotional abuse. All lost their family and roots, all were denied love and childhood happiness.

TWO BAREFOOT GIRLS DRESSED IN UNIFORM SHORT SLEEVED SHAPELESS UNBLEACHED CALLICO/OR SIMILAR SHROUDED IN WET SHEETS STANDING ON CHAIRS CENTRE STAGE.

PAM: IN CONTROL, RESILIENT.
JOAN: CONFUSED, UNHAPPY, BEWILDERED, YOUNGER.

(Off stage urgent staccato handclapping a distance away)

	PAM WHIPS THE SHEET AWAY, STEPS DOWN HASTILY SMOOTHING DRESS AND HAIR JOAN EMERGES DAZED AND TEARSTAINED FROM UNDER THE SHEET, CLIMBS DOWN UNSTEADILY PAM FOLDS HER SHEET EFFICIENTLY AND EDGES CLOSER TO JOAN
PAM:	(Quietly) Find the ends.
	JOAN STRUGGLES UNSUCCESSFULLY WITH SHEET
JOAN:	(Whispering) Can't.
	JOAN SEARCHES FEVERISHLY FOR THE ENDS
JOAN:	(Quieter whisper) It's impossible.
	PAM TOUCHES HER SHOULDER
JOAN:	(Fighting back tears) I'll never .....
PAM:	(Cutting in) Give yourself a chance. You have'nt been here two minutes! (Pause) We've all had to learn to fold: and to work the heavy pump handle in the yard. (Pause) And pump up foul rusty water

without making a fuss .....

JOAN EYES PAM QUIZZICALLY

PAM: ..... on account've the frogs and snakes.

JOAN IS HORRIFIED

PAM: There's hundreds down that well.

JOAN: Poisonous snakes?

JOAN SHRINKS INVOLUNTARILY

PAM: (Dismissive) Some.
(Long pause)
And here's a more-than-useful tip for the future.
Mealtimes, **never** push your plate away .....
... even if a plague've blowflies homed in on yesterday's mutton;
and following day's thick cold stew's alive.

JOAN: (Stifling sobs) Alive?

PAM: ... with writhing maggots.

JOAN THROWS THE SHEET TO THE GROUND

PAM: Grub's bad as that here.
(Shrugging) It's not always possible to clear the plate.

JOAN HANGS ON EVERY WORD

PAM: You learn to accept punishment.

JOAN HASTILY RETRIEVES THE SHEET

PAM: Takes a while to get to grips with institution rules and reg's.
(Pause)
Put you right, if you like?

JOAN: (Brightening) Would you?

PAM: I'm Pam.
(Long pause)
Well?

JOAN: (Hesitantly) .... Joan
(Pause)
Reverend Mother said there were more than enough Elizabeths

14

here already.
(Quietly to herself)
So she took away my real name as soon as I arrived.

PAM: Joan's as good-a-name as any .....

JOAN: But I feel like a nobody .....

PAM: ... Don't let it get to you!
Nuns don't care who any've us are:
or where we came from!

JOAN: I feel icy cold and frightened when they pass me by:
they look straight through.
I'm invisible!

PAM: Don't you believe it.

JOAN: They don't see me.

PAM: Huh! Nothing and no one escapes a nun's notice!
They've all got beady eyeballs in the back of the head.
Any of 'em will spot the teaniest weaniest hole in a sock ...
(Eyeing the skirt fabric of Joan's dress) .... the littlest stain.
Even one unimportant small word missed out've a long long
prayer ....they're all the same, nuns.

JOAN SLUMPS ONTO THE NEARER CHAIR
PAM LOOKS AROUND ANXIOUSLY TO SEE IF ANYONE
IS HEADING IN THEIR DIRECTION

PAM: (Anxiously) I'd get a move on with that sheet, Joan.

PAM RAPIDLY COMPLETES HER TASK OF FOLDING
PLACES NEATLY FOLDED SHEET ON VACANT CHAIR

JOAN: What terrible wrong did I commit to be sent away?
And why did no one want me?

PAM PUTS A FINGER TO HER LIPS

PAM: (Vehemently) Shh! Shush!

JOAN RISES TO HER FEET

JOAN: How I hate it here ...
.. Hate the nuns, hate the blistering heat and scorched earth .....

PAM: Joan!

JOAN:	.... hate the stunted dry scrubby wildness
PAM:	(Cutting in) **Joan, STOP!**
JOAN:	I **hate** everything about the place! And most've all I hate **hate** to see magpies strutting around free in the grounds, mocking me.

PAM ATTEMPTS TO HELP WITH THE SHEET

PAM:	(Hastily) The nuns'll wash your mouth out with carbolic soap!

JOAN PULLS AWAY

JOAN:	(Hysterically) I want to go **home** .....
PAM:	Joan! Listen to me!
JOAN:	Home ..... to England.

PAM HOLDS JOAN BY THE SHOULDERS TIGHTLY

PAM:	Joan, try to understand .... you're not allowed to talk like that. There are no 'reminders' here. (Pause) Everything's been 'removed' .... family photos, letters ....

PAM TAKES CHARGE OF JOAN'S SHEET

PAM:	..... presents, toys, treats, warm goodnight kisses. (Pause) All taken away from us together with names, birthdays ..... identity.
JOAN:	I don't understand any of it! I cried myself to sleep last night, Pam. I felt desperately ..... alone, unwanted.
PAM:	I used to stuff the corner of the sheet in my mouth to muffle sobs .. (Handing Joan the folded sheet and pointing to the chair) ..... the Institution is a lonely place.

JOAN MOVES TO THE CHAIR CLUTCHING SHEET

JOAN:	I'm terrified of being singled out again for bedwetting.
PAM:	(Unhappily) I was singled out, made to sleep on the outside with the wets after the first night.

And I've been there ever since.

PAM SMOOTHES DOWN JOAN'S HAIR, JOAN SMILES

PAM: (Bitterly)
I'm terrified to fall asleep at night.
(Pause)
Every day's a disappointment.
Never any different.
Up at six, dress for mass.
Stand on ...
(Gesturing)
that chair......

PAM PICKS UP A HEAVY GALVANISED BUCKET

PAM: ..... with my soiled wet sheet over my head.
For as long as it pleases Sister This or Sister That!
(Pause)
Then scrub the floor.

CARRYING THE HEAVY BUCKET CAREFULLY

PAM: And look foward to a public thrashing before bedtime.

LIFTING OUT 2 SCRUBBING BRUSHES

PAM: (Handing Joan a scrubbing brush) Promise me something, Joan?

JOAN: (Sinking to her knees) Yes!

PAM SCRUBS THE FLOOR VIGOROUSLY
JOAN WAITS FOR A RESPONSE

PAM: (Putting aside the brush)
When you sleep on the inside .... with the others.
Please be my friend.
Don't ever forget how it feels to be 'a wet'.

JOAN: I promise, cut my throat and hope to die!

PAM: Joan
(Pause)
That's what they all say.

PAM SCRUBS FURIOUSLY
JOAN SCRUBS AWKWARDLY CLOSEBY

THE BEST OF FRIENDS

VICKIE IS INCREDIBLY POPULAR AND CONFIDENT: MIDGE IS A LESS ASSURED LONER, AN EASILY OVERLOOKED BESPECTACLED UGLY DUCKLING WHO HAS NEVER EVER HAD FRIENDS, HERO WORSHIPS VICKIE AND WOULD GIVE ANYTHING TO BE VICKIE'S BEST FRIEND.

A BENCH CENTRE STAGE, MIDGE SITS EATING PACKED LUNCH ALONE AND BITES INTO A SANDWICH WITHOUT ENTHUSIASM

VICKIE:	*(Off)* Don't you dare!

LOUD CRASHING SOUND TO MIDGE'S LEFT
MIDGE TURNS AROUND SANDWICH POISED MIDAIR

VICKIE:	*(Off)* **Oh!** (Pause) You should never've done that!

MIDGE RETURNS PENSIVELY TO THE SANDWICH

VICKIE:	*(Off)* But you **stole** her from me! And you know it.

MIDGE LAYS THE HALF EATEN SANDWICH DOWN
CAUTIOUSLY STANDS INTENDING TO CREEP NEAR

ENTER. VICKIE: UPSET

VICKIE:	(To Lisa offstage) She was **my** best friend! How **could** you, Lisa?

MIDGE FREEZES GUILTILY CAUGHT IN THE ACT
SITS HASTILY, STARING WIDE EYED AT VICKIE

VICKIE:	Well, Midge?
MIDGE:	Wwwhat?
VICKIE:	What you staring at?
MIDGE:	Nnnnothing.
VICKIE:	Listening, were you? Heard everything, did you?

MIDGE SHAKES HEAD IN AN EMPHATIC DENIAL

MIDGE: I...I, eer...

VICKIE: Don't bother with excuses:
                the whole school will be full've it soon enough, anyway.

MIDGE: I...I don't know what you're on about, Vickie.

VICKIE: **Really?**
                Well! That was Lisa getting lairy, back there for your
                information.
                She called my mother a name.
                (Pause)
                .... over Sarah.
                (Pause)
                (Bitterly) Lisa took Sarah away.
                She took her away from me.
                And I **hate** her for that.

MIDGE: (Frightened to speak) ..... Sssarah?

VICKIE: We've broken friends.

MIDGE: Yyou're not best friends with Sarah any more?

                VICKIE SITS ON THE END OF THE BENCH

VICKIE: (Impatiently) Haven't I just told you?
                Sarah's gone off with Lisa.

MIDGE: Oh..h!

VICKIE: (Suspiciously) You're not friends with that Lisa?
                ..... Are you?

MIDGE: (Quickly) Nnno!

                MIDGE SCRABBLES THROUGH THE LUNCHBOX
                OFFERS VICKIE A CHOCOLATE BAR

VICKIE: ..... Or friends with Sarah, neither?

MIDGE: Nno.....Vickie!

VICKIE: (Taking the bar) .....Thought as much.

                MIDGE FIDGETS UNEASILY

MIDGE: (Hastily shutting lunchbox) Best be going, I ssuppose.

MIDGE JUMPS UP NERVOUSLY

VICKIE:	Midge, wait. There's something .....
MIDGE:	(Cutting in) Wwhat? (Pause) You want me to say I haven't got a best friend; that I haven't got even a friend at all. Ttthat no one wants to be my friend.

VICKIE:　　(Standing) Wanna be friends with me?

MIDGE STANDS CLUTCHING LUNCH BOX

VICKIE:　　Well?

MIDGE NODS AWKWARDLY

MIDGE:　　Bbbut I thought you spread it around that I was boring.

VICKIE:　　(Chanting) Make friends, make friends
Never, never break friends.
(Pause)
Midge .....(Whispers in Midge's ear)

MIDGE:　　(Laughs nervously) No! I can't see without them.

VICKIE LINKS ARMS WITH MIDGE
MIDGE CATCHES SIGHT OF SARAH ..... FALTERS

MIDGE:　　(Pointing) Vickie!
Sarah's over there.

VICKIE:　　Wanna look your best?
(Removing Midge's spectacles)
MIDGE:　　(Cutting in) Ggggive them bbback .....

VICKIE:　　Wait here.

VICKIE HESITATES, HANDS SPECTACLES BACK

EXIT VICKIE.

VICKIE:　　*(Off)* Sarah! Make friends?
(Pause)
Me! Friends with that little sneak Midge? **Please!**

MIDGE REPLACES SPECTACLES, TURNS AWAY SAD

20

THREE WAY CONVERSATION

BEE AND ALEX BICKER OVER ANYTHING AND EVERYTHING BUT TELEPHONE HOGGING GUARANTEES A MAJOR FIGHT.

ALEX SPRAWLES IN AN ARMCHAIR CENTRE STAGE, LEGS DANGLING OVER ONE ARM, A TELEPHONE SET HANGING FROM ONE HAND, RECEIVER CRADLED BETWEEN HEAD AND SHOULDER (FREEING ONE HAND FOR EXPRESSIVE GESTURE) ENGROSSED IN A LONG PHONE CALL.

ALEX:	Mmmm .....
	(Pausing to listen)
	Masses and masses.
	(Pausing to listen)
	(Sighing loudly)
	'S'pose I really-auta-be slaving away
	Instead've gabbing.'
	(Listening whilst placing the telephone set on the floor
	and snuggling down more comfortably)
	Mmm.
	Tell me 'bout it!
	Always.
	Talk about full scale production number!
	There's always a drama over the phone bill.
	You'd think I was the only person around here
	who'd learnt to dial out.

BEE IS HEARD IN AN ADJOINING ROOM

BEE:	*(Off)* **Alex!**
ALEX:	(Quietly) Gotta go, Fran.
BEE:	*(Off)* **Alex!**
ALEX:	No! Nothing to do with **that!**
	(Hissed whisper)
	Bee's on the warpath, that's why.
BEE:	*(Off)* Don't tell me you're on the phone, **again**!

ALEX SCOOPS UP TELEPHONE AND CLUTCHES
HANDSET AND RECEIVER TIGHT AS BEE BURSTS IN

ENTER. BEE: STRIDING ACROSS IMMEDIATELY TO THE ARMCHAIR

ALEX:	(Casting anxious glance over one shoulder)
	Forget 'What-I-Just-Said' ...

21

BEE:	(Triumphantly) You **are! I knew** it.

ALEX: ..... My mistake!
It's Attila the Hun making a personal guest appearance.
Not 'Who-I-Said-It-Was' before!

BEE GLARES AT ALEX SUSPICIOUSLY

ALEX: *(To Bee)* Fran says Attila the Hun was an exeptionally foul
unpleasant, smelly, cruel and ugly historical character.
Agree?

ALEX WAVES THE RECEIVER. IN BEE'S DIRECTION
BEE GLARES SILENTLY WITHOUT RESPONDING

ALEX: Hear that, Fran?
(Listening)
Right!..... No opinion .....
(Listening and laughing aloud)
I could 'name that person', too!
(Staring hard at Bee)
That 'certain person' who couldn't work it out in a trillion .....

BEE: (Cutting in) Alex! I need the phone .....
ALEX: (Cutting in) ..... trillion trillion light years .
BEE: (Cutting in) ......**Right now!**

BEE CLOSES IN THREATENINGLY

ALEX: Did you hear, Fran?
(Mocking)
Bee needs to make a call.
(Cowering) I'd better hang up ..... s'pose.
(Pausing to listen)
Mmmmmm ..... really-auta.

BEE CIRCLES THE ARMCHAIR MENACINGLY

ALEX: .....Mmmm ..... Causing me grief.
(Pausing to listen)
..... 'Fraid so, 'fraid so.
(Laughing aloud)

BEE: You and your precious friend Fran.

ALEX: *(To Bee)* What?

BEE: Think I'm fair game, don't you?

ALEX:	(Shrugging shoulders) Anyone would think we were slagging you off, Bee.
BEE:	I know what you two cherub's from hell are at! Just stay out've my sight ..... **for ever!** Or else! You tell Fran from me.
ALEX:	Bee says we're a right pair of 'fat satanic babes'. And would prefer not to meet up with us for a while. (Listening and pulling a face) (*To Bee)* Fran says the feeling's mutual.

BEE SNATCHES THE TELEPHONE AND RECEIVER

BEE:	(*To Fran*) **Fran!**
ALEX:	(Cutting in) **How dare you!** Fran's **my** friend
BEE:	(*To Fran)* Now! You listen to me.
ALEX:	You **can't** talk to Fran: I don't want you to. Give it back .

ALEX TRIES TO SNATCH THE RECEIVER AWAY

BEE:	(*To Fran)* Can't hear a word! Speak up. Speak up. **Speak up!** **SPEAK UP!**

ALEX JUMPS UP AND BEE STEALS ALEX'S PLACE

ALEX:	I'm telling!

BEE SETTLES COMFORTABLY, DANGLES LEGS
AND KICKS OFF SHOES AS ALEX RUSHES AWAY

ALEX:	**Mum! MUM!**

EXIT ALEX.

BEE REPLACES THE RECEIVER CAREFULLY

ALEX:	(*Off)* Bee's been on the phone for absolutely ages and ages! What about the phone bill, Eh?

THE ROW

LISA HAS FALLEN OUT WITH BEST AND ONLY FRIEND VANDELLA
BARNSDORF OVER A FRIENDSHIP WITH ROBERT THE NEW BOY IN
CLASS. 'VAN' AN INSULAR OPINIONATED FEMINIST IS OVER
INDULGED BY LIBERAL PARENTS AND LOATHES BOYS. LISA IS SHY,
PERFORMS WELL AT SCHOOL AND HAS BEEN UNFAIRLY LABELLED
BRAINY AND SNOBBISH BY HER PEER GROUP.

LISA, A YOUNG THIRTEEN CONSIDERS HERSELF UNATTRACTIVE IN THE
EXTREME TO THE OPPOSITE SEX AND DRESSES AND BEHAVES IN AN
UNOBTRUSIVE NATURAL MANNER. VAN IS PHYSICALLY MATURE, WAY
AHEAD OF FAR-OUT FASHION, AND HAS ADOPTED HER FATHER'S
OVERSIZED KNITTED JACKET TO MASK A WEIGHT PROBLEM.

(N.B. VAN SPEAKS WITH A PRONOUNCED SOUTHERN DRAWL IF AMERICAN ACCENTS
ARE USED)

VAN (FLOUTING AUTHORITY), LEANS BACK IN A CHAIR, FEET UP ON
A TABLE FLIPPING THROUGH AN OFF-BEAT PUBLICATION.

ENTER. LISA: HURRIDLY

LISA:	Van, I need you to do me a favour.

VAN THROWS DOWN THE PUBLICATION AND MOVES
OFF DELIBERATELY TURNING HER BACK ON LISA

VAN:	(Over one shoulder) What?
LISA:	I want you to pass Robert a note in Mrs Cronski's class..... (Van turns to confront Lisa) ..... telling him to meet you during lunchbreak in the alley behind the school. (Pause) (Biting her lip) Only instead of you it'll be me.
VAN:	(Frostily) Anything else?

THEY SUFFER AN UNCOMFORTABLE SILENCE

LISA:	(With resignation) You're not going to do it, are you?
VAN:	(Aggressively) Why should I?
LISA:	Because I'm trying to keep Robert from getting himself expelled.

24

VAN:	(Sniffing) Doesn't matter to me. (Shrugging) (Aside) Just one less of the **ENEMY** to deal with when he leaves.
LISA:	(Intensly) Knock it off!
VAN:	(Shouting back aggressively) Knock what off?
	LISA TAKES A STEP BACK AND THEY PAUSE TO TAKE BREATH AND EVALUATE THE SITUATION
LISA:	(Calmly) Why is Robert so particularly bad?
VAN:	(Rolling her eyes & sighing loudly) Come on! Just look at all the trouble he's in.
LISA:	That doesn't answer my question.
VAN:	(Pressing her lips tightly together) I **did** answer your question.
LISA:	What do you find so wrong with him?
VAN:	(Sighing loudly) I find wrong with him what everybody else finds wrong. He always pretends to be somebody else ..... usually somebody who was great and famous. Well! (Pause) He's **not** those other people ..... (Pause) ..... And he's **not** great and famous. He's just plain Robert Wormer. (Shrugging shoulders) So why doesn't he just **be** Robert Wormer?
LISA:	(Sarcastically) So why don't **you** just be plain Vandelle Barnsdorf, then?
VAN:	**HUH?**
LISA:	No one in the school is dressed like you. Why do you mess with your hair And wear all of those weird clothes?
VAN:	Because I'm an individual.

That ought to be clear even to you.
(Pause)
(Haughtily) I'm making a statement
about women in general
and **me** specifically.

LISA: Really!

VAN: That we can dress how we want;
when we want.
And should not be discriminated against for it.
For the good of our sex
we've got to stay on the offensive.

LISA: (Softly) Then why are you wearing that?
(Touching the sleeve of Van's unbuttoned knitted jacket)

VAN: (Tightly wrapping the 2 sides protectively around herself)
I'm cold.
(Pause)
I'ts been cold these last few days.....
.....usually happens in the wintertime.

LISA: It's spring, Van.
The days are getting warmer, not colder.

VAN: (Defensively) Well!
Maybe I'm having trouble with my internal thermostat.
(Aggressively) How should I know?
(Pause)
I'm just cold, that's all.

LISA: Van, it's okay if you're worried about .....

VAN HALF TURNS AND LISA BLOCKS AN ESCAPE

LISA: ..... How heavy you are.

VAN: (Aggressively) I'm **not** worried.

LISA: **Van** .....
.....Van. You pretend just as much as Robert does.

VAN: (Shouting) **What!**

LISA: (Icily) **You do!** It's like my mother said .....

VAN:	(Sarcastically) **Oh!** Your .... **mother**. She doing your thinking for you now?
LISA:	**No!** (With rising anger) Why don't you admit that you wear those clothes to cover up your weight.
VAN:	(Hysterically) I do **not!**
LISA:	You pretend to be this great feminist when you really wish you were slim and could date boys like anybody else!
VAN:	You're **crazy!**
LISA:	(Words tumbling fast) But that's not the worst part. The worst part isn't pretending that.

VAN HANGS HER HEAD

LISA:	(Choking back tears) .... **Van!** The worst part is pretending .... not to like me.
VAN:	(Emotionally) I **don't** like you, Lisa.
LISA:	You do!
VAN:	**Don't! Don't! Don't!**
LISA:	**You do**! And I think that's the worst thing you could ever do to someone who considered you a friend. (Staring Van hard in the eyes) ..... A **best** friend.

THEY CONFRONT EACH OTHER BREATHING HARD
VAN BITES LIP, TUGS NERVOUSLY AT HER JACKET

VAN:	(Quietly) I'll give him the note.

LISA HANDS VAN THE NOTE FROM A POCKET
VAN WALKS OFF WITHOUT ANY SIGN OF EMOTION

LISA:	(Emotionally) It hurt, Van.
VAN:	(Quietly without turning) I'll give him the note.

EXIT VAN.

LISA: It really hurt.

The Row is adapted from chapter 11
'Taking Off' by Joseph McNair
By permission of Macmillan Children's Books

PEARS

THE DRESS REHEARSAL HAD PROVED TO BE A DISASTROUS FIASCO DESPITE THE BEAUTIFUL HISTORICAL COSTUMES/FULL LENGTH EVENING WEAR. THE CAST IS 'TAKING FIVE' BACKSTAGE PRIOR TO AN INEVITABLE COMPLETE RUN THROUGH.

ENTER. MEL AND IZZY: DOWNCAST, DRINKING FROM PAPER CUPS

> MEL THROWS DOWN HER EMPTY CUP, LIFTS SKIRTS
> AND TRAMPLES ON THE CUP AGGRESSIVELY

MEL: Izzy, anyone'd think it was **our** fault
that the whole thing was a disaster.
(Sweeping backwards and fowards)
If only Jo hadn'tve collided with me.
I wouldn'tve pushed you.
And you wouldn'tve fallen over
and tripped up Hannah.

IZZY: Actually, everything was going more or less brilliantly
until Laura turned up.

MEL: (Bitchily) Darling Laura, late again!
Huh! Makes a change.

IZZY: (To herself) I don't think!

> IZZY WANDERS OVER TO A WASTE BIN

MEL: More's the pity she bothered at all!

IZZY: She's missed most rehearsals altogether,
doesn't have a clue what's going on half the time.
I'm only surprised she turned up today.

MEL: Izzy, this is the full dress:
she had'ta show her face.

IZZY: Laura should never've been picked in the first place.
Mel.

> IZZY TAKES AIM, THROWS CUP INTO THE WASTE BIN
> AND SAUNTERS BACK

MEL: (Applauding)
The audition was 'fixed'.

29

Surprise, surprise!

IZZY: Actually, Amy's pretty useless, too.

MEL: You can say that again.
            (Holding two fingers close) And who is Amy like that with?

IZZY: Laura!

MEL: 'nuf said! Izzy.
            That explains everything.

IZZY: Like why Laura and Amy are at the front?
MEL: (Cutting in) Where they can be seen by everyone .....

IZZY: ..... and we're hidden from sight in the wings all the time.

MEL: Or pushed to the back.
            Huh!

IZZY: I thought Laura and Amy've been doing classes for longer than
            any of us, but somewhere else.

MEL: They might have.
            So?

IZZY: So, that's why.

MEL: (Shrugging)   But they're not as good.

IZZY: Miss Cathy thinks they are.

MEL: (Conspiratorally) Not necessarily.

IZZY: Then why did Miss Cathy bring them in half way through
            rehearsals and stand them right at the front?

MEL: Because've their mothers.

IZZY: What about their mothers?

            MEL SHRUGS NONCOMMITTALLY

IZZY: Don't hold out on me!
            (Pleading) Tell me!

MEL: Can't.

IZZY:	Mel. You can tell me!
MEL:	My Mum and your Mum were jawing outside the school. I only heard bits and pieces, mind you.
IZZY:	Like?
MEL:	Everything'd gone pearshaped.
IZZY:	**Pearshaped?**
MEL:	..... After Laura and Amy had been added. That ....
IZZY:	(Cutting in) Mel, You sure you've got this right?
MEL:	Yeah!
IZZY:	Only my Mum's always moaning about her figure. Says she's pearshaped.
MEL:	Next you'll be saying your Mum was asking my Mum to buy a bag of pears.
IZZY:	No! Anyway, there'd be no point.
MEL:	(Suspiciously) Why?
IZZY:	We only eat tinned! Boom! Boom!
MEL:	Izzy. Save it for the panto.
IZZY:	Anyway. What's any of this got to do with pears.
MEL:	Nothing whatsoever. My understanding of it was ..... (Pause) .... that Amy's Laura's new friend and Laura's Mum is Miss Cathy's sister: Laura and her Mum've come over to live and they're staying at Amy's Mum's.
IZZY:	You don't say?
MEL:	Something like that!
IZZY:	Mel?

31

Are you having me on?

MEL: (Gleefully) **Yes!**
Truth is ....
you and me're ..... **rubbish.**
(Pause)
(Curtsying) Laura and Amy are stars:

IZZY: (Curtsying) And we're a right pair.

MEL:} Boom! Boom!
IZZY:}

MEL: It's a rotten production.

IZZY: Hey!
Let's leave everyone to it.

EXIT: MEL AND IZZY.

BULLIES

NIT IS AN ISOLATE AND LOOKS DIFFERENT (EITHER ETHNIC MINORITY MEMBER/AN OBVIOUS PHYSICAL DISABILITY E.G. PRONOUNCED LIMP, OVERWEIGHT, UNDERSIZED/WEARING UNFASHIONABLE CLOTHES THREE SIZES TOO LARGE). NIT IS STANDING AT A BUS STOP AFTER SCHOOL SPLATTERED WITH MUD FROM HEAD TO FOOT.

ENTER. JODY: EMBARRASSED AT COMING FACE TO FACE WITH NIT

JODY:	(Eventually) What happened, Nit?
NIT:	(Shrugging and fighting back tears) Fell over again, didn't I? (Pause) Arn't you going to have a good laugh, then?
JODY:	You never fell.

NIT TRIES TO REGAIN COMPOSURE

JODY:	Nit.

NIT STARES DOWN AT THE GROUND

JODY:	Picking on you again, right?
NIT:	What's it to you, Jody?
JODY:	Don't you really mind being called Nit by everyone?
NIT:	What do you think? How would you like it? (Long pause) That's how it started with them calling me names. Nit stuck. An' that's that. Nothink I can do about any've it.
JODY:	They've gone too far, this time; look at the state you're in.
NIT:	They picked on me from day one. First it was the way they looked at me. Wanted me to loose my rag. Didn't they?

(Pause)
Put me down, all the time.
Called me names.
Called me Mum a name an'all.
An' that was just the start.

JODY: Your Mum'll be up the school, tomorrow.
They'll all be excluded.
You see.

NIT: (Cutting in) For five days.
What's the good in that?
Five days, then they'll be back.
Ganging up on me. Beating me up.
It just gets worse all the time.
Don't you understand?

JODY IS EMBARRASSED, LOOKS AT WRISTWATCH

JODY: I'm off!

NIT: What?

JODY: I'm going t' walk, aren't I?

NIT: You don't want to be seen talking.
That's the truth of it.
You're frightened they'll see;
and start on you.
(Pause)
(Quietly) It's all got too much for me, Jody.
I can't face going to school: can't face going home.
I can't go on like it.

JODY: (Hastily) Bye, Nit.

NIT: (Shouting after Jody) If people like you stood up to them
things would be different.
Come back.
Please, Jody.
Stay.
Sit with me on the bus.
Please, Jody. Please.
(Pause)
(Screaming) **Jody!**
You're as bad as them and I hate you just as much!

EXIT JODY.

34

HEADLINES

EM IS STRUGGLING TO DO HOMEWORK ONE END OF A SMALL TABLE PILED HIGH WITH LOOSE SHEETS OF PAPERS, FILES AND A FOLDED NEWSPAPER. EM CONSULTS A HUGE TEXTBOOK AND TRANSFERS INFORMATION INTO AN EXCERCISE BOOK WITH A GREAT DEAL OF CROSSING OUT.
EM NEEDS TO WORK HARD TO ACHIEVE, ALWAYS TRIES AND TAKES LIFE SERIOUSLY WHILST JESS IS MORE OUTGOING WITH A RELAXED ATTITUDE, BOTH ARE DRESSED IN SCHOOL UNIFORM.

A TABLE & 2 DINING CHAIRS CENTRE STAGE AND AN ARMCHAIR TO ONE SIDE.

ENTER. JESS: BREEZILY.

JESS:	How goes the physics?
EM:	Don't ask.
	JESS PEERS OVER EM'S SHOULDER PULLS A FACE
EM:	(Shielding exercise book) **Jess!**
JESS:	Pardon me!
EM:	**Go away!**
JESS:	There's no need to bite my head off!
EM:	Can't you see I'm busy.
	JESS SNATCHES THE NEWSPAPER FROM THE TABLE EM TRIES BUT FAILS TO PREVENT JESS TAKING IT
JESS:	(Waving the newspaper in the air) You won't be needing this then.
	JESS THROWS HIM/HERSELF INTO THE ARMCHAIR EM TRIES TO CONCENTRATE WHILST JESS NOISILY CRUMPLES AND TURNS PAGES
EM:	**Jess!**
JESS:	What?
EM:	Are you going out of your way to annoy me?

35

| JESS: | Don't know what you're on about. |
| | I haven't uttered a single word. |

EM:	(Accusingly) **You!**
	Were rustling pages on purpose.
	And you know it.

| JESS: | **Please!** |
| | Do me a favour. |

EM WRITES NOTES AND CONSULTS THE TEXTBOOK
JESS READS THE NEWSPAPER IN ABSOLUTE SILENCE

JESS:	(Reading aloud)
	'Emu shells hold clue to Ice Age'
EM:	(Cutting in angrily)
	Cut it out!
JESS:	Knock me down with a feather!
	'..... Fossil emu eggshells have shown
	that Ice Age conditions in the northern hemisphere
	triggered cooling around the globe.'
	Well!

EM:	**Riveting!**
	Makes about as much sense as .....
	(Holding textbook aloft)
	..... this bookload of squiggles.

JESS DUCKS BEHIND THE NEWSPAPER

EM:	**Jess!**
	Can't you leave me to get on with my work
	for a minute?

EM FLICKS THROUGH THE TEXTBOOK ANGRILY

JESS:	(Reading aloud)
	'The future's dark'
	'When all the stars have burnt out,
	the universe will remain for ever dark,
	empty and meaningless .....'

EM CREEPS UP AND SNATCHES THE NEWSPAPER

| JESS: | **Em!** |

| EM: | Guess your immediate future looks pretty empty and |
| | meaningless, now! |

JESS:	(Smiling) You win.

JESS HURRIES OVER TO SIT AT THE TABLE AND
IMMEDIATELY SORTS OUT PAPERS METHODICALLY
EM 'S ATTENTION IS CAUGHT BY A HEADLINE

EM:	(Reading aloud) **'Bird hits riders'** (Pause) 'Dr Gillian McRay was in critical condition after being hit by a chicken that flew out of a hedge while she was riding with her husband David .....

JESS:	Shh!

EM:	..... on a tandem bicycle.'

EM SINKS INTO THE ARMCHAIR LOST IN THE
NEWSPAPER

JESS:	Shhhh! Some of us are trying to work around here.

STAGESTRUCK

GUM CHEWING MAX LACKS CONCENTRATION AND ADE IS EASILY LED SO THE BEST FRIENDS SPEND THEIR TIME HANGING AROUND PLACES OR DRIFTING AIMLESSLY, CONSEQUENTLY THEY HAVE FOUND THEMSELVES IN TROUBLE ON INNUMERABLE OCCASIONS AND ARE NOW ANXIOUS TO AVOID A THREATENED PUNISHMENT

A HIGH BACKED CHAIR AND OPEN TRUNK WITH RAISED LID NEARBY 'THE WRONG WAY ROUND' i.e. BACKS FACING FRONT STAGE (THE SCENE IS LITERALLY PLAYED FRONT TO BACK) MAX, A FAST NERVOUS TALKER AND ADE HOLD AN ANIMATED CONVERSATION OFF STAGE.

MAX:	*(Off)* Why not?	
ADE:	*(Off)* Don't think we should? That's why!	
MAX:	*(Off)* There's no one about to know is there?	
ADE:	*(Off)* You go; if you're so keen, Max.	

ENTER. MAX: PEERING CHEEKILY FROM THE WINGS, STEPPING OUT WITH ADOPTED OUTWARD DONT CARE ATTITUDE

MAX:	(Beckoning) Come on! (Walking backwards) Ade! **Ade!**
ADE:	*(Off)* (hesitantly) I'm not so sure.
MAX:	Where's the harm?

MAX DISCOVERS A BOOK ON THE CHAIR SEAT
FLICKS THROUGH ALL THE WHILE CHEWING GUM

ENTER. ADE: HEAD EMERGING CAUTIOUSLY FROM THE WINGS

ADE:	(Nervous whisper) What are you doing?
MAX:	What's it look like? Reading!

ADE TIP-TOES OUT CAUTIOUSLY
MAX RUNS OVER AND LOBS THE BOOK AT ADE

MAX:	Catch!

MAX MIMES A FENCING DUEL ENTHUSIASTICALLY
TAKES A BOW 'THE WRONG WAY ROUND' WHILE
ADE PERCHES ON A CHAIR ARM, OPENS THE BOOK

ADE: (Quietly to him/herself)
Full fathom five thy father lies .....

MAX: Nothing much happening around here.
Time to move on, Ade.
Fancy a burger and fries?
(Blowing a huge bubble)

ADE: Listen to this, Max.
(Reading aloud Ariel's Song, The Tempest, Shakespeare
or preferred text of your choice)
Full fathom five thy father lies.
(Max bursts the gum bubble)
Of his bones are coral made.
(Max chews impatiently)

MAX: I've listened!
I'm hungry, lets go.

ADE: Those are pearls that were his eyes .....
MAX: (Cutting in) Enough!
(Max blows a bubble)
ADE: ..... Nothing of him that doth fade,
But doth suffer a sea-change
MAX: (Cutting in) Come on! Come on! Come on!
ADE: (Closing book) Into something rich ...
(Max bursts the bubble)
... and strange .....
MAX: (Cutting in) I'm on my way.
Ade? For the very last time've asking:
are you coming or not?

ADE STANDS WITH BACK TO MAX (i.e. facing front)
MAX PACES BACKWARDS AND FOWARDS

ADE: (Over shoulder) What's the hurry?

MAX: (Laughing) You stage struck or something, Ade?

ADE: (Turning to Max) No one's asking you to stay.

MAX: What's got into you?

ADE HEADS FOR THE TRUNK

MAX HESITATES AT A LOSS, FINALLY TURNS AWAY

ADE: (Opening the book) Sea-nymphs ...

MAX: I'm gone!

ADE: (Smiling) Sea-nymphs
hourly ring his knell .....

ADE LAYS DOWN THE BOOK AND PICKS UP A
HAND HELD MASK FROM THE TRUNK

MAX: (Turning back) Ade!
What are you up to?
You'll be in dead trouble if you're caught up on stage
rummaging around ...

ADE: ..... Hark!

MAX: I'm out've here.
(Pointing a finger) You're pushing your luck
and well you know it;
don't blame me when they catch up with you.

ADE: (Sarcastically) Hark!
Now I hear them .....

ADE HOLDS UP MASK TO FACE
MAX STORMS OFF

EXIT MAX.

ADE: (Ghostly chant) ..... Ding-dong bell.
Ding-dong bell ...
Ding-dong-ding-dong ...

MAX: *(Off)* Ade! Scarper: someone's coming!

ADE DROPS THE MASK AND RUNS

EXIT ADE.

MAX: *(Off)* (Laughing)
Only joking, Ade.

HOUDINI'S HOUSE

A SETTEE/2 ARMCHAIRS PUSHED CLOSE TOGETHER WITH A TINY OCCASIONAL TABLE TUCKED UP TIGHT AGAINST ONE ARM, FRONT STAGE. MO IN NIGHTCLOTHES NESTLING IN CUSHIONS AND LEX, IN CASUAL DRESS, PERCHED ON THE OTHER ARM, HAS JUST FINISHED READING MO A CONSIDERABLE NUMBER OF BEDTIME STORIES.

> **LEX: AN OLDER CHILD LOVES BOOKS, READS EXCEPTIONALLY WELL AND EXPRESSIVELY**
> **MO: CONSIDERABLY YOUNGER LOVES TO HEAR BEDTIME STORIES, IS LIVELY, A LITTLE DEVIOUS AND ALWAYS PUSHES BOUNDARIES**

LEX:　　(Snapping the book shut) Bedtime!

MO:　　　One more.
(Pause)
One more, just one more.
Pleese, Lex!

LEX:　　But it's way past bedtime.

MO:　　　I'll go straight to bed on my own without being asked.
(Pause)
If you read me one more!
Promise!
Lex.
Pleese!
The book's almost finished;
there's only the one story left.
You **never** read that one!
Read it to me!
Pleeeese!

MO MAKES AN UNSUCCESSFUL GRAB FOR THE
BOOK AS LEX HOLDS IT OUT AT ARMS LENGTH

LEX:　　Ttt! Ttt! Ttt!
Too scarey.
It's scarey, little Mo.

MO:　　　It's not! It's **not!**

LEX:　　How would you know?

MO:　　　(Sulkily) What makes it so scarey, then?

LEX:　　(Spookily) **Ghosts!** Spooks!
Things that go bump-in-the-night!

MO:	I'm not scared. (Leaning over) Lex, what's the last story called?
LEX:	'Houdini's House'
	MO SETTLES COMFORTABLY EXPECTING LEX TO READ AND IS DISAPPOINTED BUT REFUSES TO GIVE UP AND LEANS OVER AND TUGS LEX'S SLEEVE
MO:	(Puzzled) Who is Houdini?
LEX:	Who **was** Houdini? (Fondly) He was a magician and the world's greatest ever escapologist .....
MO:	(Cutting in) Pardon?
LEX:	Esca ... pologist.
MO:	(Suspiciously) What's an excaploganist .....?
LEX:	(Cutting in) Someone who escapes from inside locked safes and trunks.
MO:	(Wide eyed) Houdini did that?
LEX:	He could escape from anything, anywhere. Even from inside a padlocked mailbag, with handcuffed wrists ankles bound with rope, hung upside down in a full tank of water. (Pause) Houdini could hold his breath under water for longer than anyone. He **always** managed to free himself.
MO:	(Anxiously) Lex. What happened to him?
LEX:	Houdini cheated death again and again many many times.
MO:	Then?
LEX:	He fell ill ..... (Long Pause) one Halloween......
MO:	(Squirming) Is Houdini a ghost now?

A ghost in his own house?
Is Houdini's House a true story?

LEX: (Opening the book) Only one way to find out, Mo.

MO: Perhaps it is a little late for a story.

MO CURLS UP

LEX: (Reading) 'The old shuttered house had a deserted mystical air
and dark dark atmosphere that rose up from the cellar
and touched the attic and hung over the high gables......'

MO: (Cutting in) Lex, it's my bedtime.

LEX: '..... A bleak icy moon .....'

MO: (Cutting in) Lex ...

LEX: '....veiled by scudding clouds ..'

MO: (Cutting in) Lex!

LEX: '... mirrored in blind window panes .... '

MO: (Cutting in) I'm sleepy ....

LEX: 'and the midnight air heavy with magic and whispered secrets.
My eye was drawn to .....'

MO: (Cutting in) I'm sleepy .....

LEX: '....a tarnished plaque set high above the door
...in the wall of that bizarre rambling house.'

MO: (Cutting in) I'm too sleepy.

LEX: *'HOUDINI * THE FINAL CURTAIN FELL *
HALLOWEEN NIGHT 1926'*
I froze. A chilling shiver ran down my spine.
This was the night of the anniversary of Houdini's death.
(Turning the page)
I found myself drawn closer to the house, against my will ..'

MO: (Sleepily) Don't want a story!

LEX: '.. my heart pounding, throat dry.
I fought to quell a terrible sense of foreboding
as I climbed the flight of worn stone steps ...'

MO SNUGGLES DOWN EYES CLOSED FEIGNING SLEEP
LEX GROWS INCREASINGLY INVOLVED IN THE BOOK

LEX: '... that led up from the deserted pavement
to a substantial black door with curious heavy
elephant head door knocker .....'

MO KNOCKS LOUDLY ON THE COFFEE TABLE
LEX SHOOTS UP, SCREAMS AND DROPS THE BOOK

AND RUNS OFF IN TERROR

EXIT LEX.

MO: Lex?
        Aren't you going to finish the story?

        MO LAUGHS, YAWNS AND SNUGGLES BACK DOWN

PEACE

ARISTOPHANES COMIC ALLEGORY DESCRIBES THE EFFORTS OF ELDERLY FARMER TRYGAEUS TO RETURN PEACE TO ATHENS BY FLYING UP TO HEAVEN ON THE BACK OF A GIANT DUNG -BEETLE ('WINGED STEED'!) TO GAIN A PRIVATE AUDIENCE WITH ZEUS

THE SAVAGE PLAY WAS FIRST PERFORMED IN 421 BC AND REFLECTS THE ANGUISH AND DESPAIR OF ATHENIANS LEFT WITHOUT HOPE AFTER TEN YEARS UNDER SIEGE. ARISTOPHANES WORK IS CYNICAL ABOUT THE GODS AND DEMAGOGUES AND PROVIDES THE VEHICLE FOR A VITRIOLIC RETROSPECTIVE ATTACK ON ATHENIAN LEADER CLEON WHOSE SELF INTEREST HAD INVARIABLY OUTWEIGHED DESIRE FOR PEACE AND FREEDOM FOR ATHENS AND HER PEOPLE.

N.B. This extract from Peace may be played as slapstick comedy/pantomime routine

A FARMYARD OUTSIDE ATHENS, BALE OF HAY (OR BENCH) CENTRE STAGE.
A LARGE STABLE WITH HALF-DOOR BEYOND THE LINE OF VISION.
BAREFOOT SLAVES WEARING HEAVILY STAINED OVERSIZE COOK'S APRONS.

> **SLAVE 1: BRIGHT, CHEERFUL, QUICK ON THE UPTAKE**
> **SLAVE 2: PONDEROUS, STRAIGHT-FACED, INDECISIVE**

SLAVE 1 LISTENS OUT BEFORE HURRYING ACROSS

SLAVE 1:   Come on! Come on!
(Beckoning frantically)
Hurry up!
Quick! Another pancake.
Hurry!

> *SOUND OF RESTLESS WEIGHTY BODY CRASHING*
> *AGAINST STABLE DOOR.*
> SLAVE1 BECKONS FRANTICALLY

SLAVE 1:   (Aside) The beetle's still hungry.

ENTER. SLAVE 2: STAGGERING UNDER THE WEIGHT OF AN ENORMOUS COWPAT

SLAVE 2:   (Offering the cowpat) Hhhere you are!

SLAVE 1:   (Side-stepping) You give it, him!
(Pulling a face) Abominable brute.

SLAVE 2:   I'hhhope h'es bitten off more than he can chew.

SLAVE 2 HURLS THE COWPAT INTO THE STABLE

SLAVE 2:	I hhhhope it's the sweetest daintiest morsel he ever tastes.

GREEDY SNUFFLES AND GRUNTS FROM STABLE
SLAVE 2 RETREATS NERVOUSLY

SLAVE 1:	You'd better go and make another.
SLAVE 2:	(Mouth falling open) Another?
SLAVE 1:	(Clapping hands) Another. (Pause) And make the next ....**bigger**, more substantial.
SLAVE 2:	(Dispirited) Mmmore mmore mmore.

SLAVE 2 TURNS AROUND OBEDIENTLY

SLAVE 1:	But go see what happened to the last one, first.

SLAVE 2 TURNS FULL CIRCLE DESPONDENTLY
AND TIPTOES TOWARDS THE STABLE

EXIT SLAVE 2.

SLAVE 1:	(Shouting) Can'tve eaten that already. Has he?

ENTER. SLAVE 2: IN SHOCKED STATE

SLAVE 2:	Ccccouldn't even wait to chew it. Rrrolled-it-into-a-ball with two feet and-bbbolted-it-down in one!

SLAVE1 REGISTERS DISBELIEF, STRIDES TO STABLE

EXIT SLAVE 1.

SLAVE 1:	(Popping head out) Pancake mix! (Clapping hands) Quick! (Withdrawing head)
SLAVE 2:	**(Aside)** Oh! Heaven help me or I'll ccchoke and die! The sssstench will be the death of me!
SLAVE 1:	(Popping head out) Another pancake! **Bring him another**. (Clapping hands, withdrawing head)
SLAVE 2:	**(Aside)** I'll die in front of you!

LOUD CRASHING SOUNDS FROM THE STABLE

ENTER. SLAVE 1:

    SLAVE 1:   Stop wasting time.

    SLAVE 2 WALKS OFF SULKILY

    SLAVE 2:   (Muttering) Annnother annother another.
                   Another more finely moulded perhaps?

                                         EXIT SLAVE 2.

ENTER. SLAVE 2: STAGGERING UNDER THE WEIGHT OF HUGE COWPAT

    SLAVE 2:   Hhhere it is.
                   (Sniffing the cowdung)
                   (Aside) There's only one good thing to be said for this job.
                   Nnno-one will accuse me of licking spoons
                   or picking at the food.

    SLAVE 1 RUSHES OVER AND SNATCHES COWPAT

                           EXIT SLAVE 1. INTO STABLE

    SLAVE 2 PLODS OFF MECHANICALLY TO FETCH
    ANOTHER COWPAT

ENTER. SLAVE 1: HASTILY

    SLAVE 1:   More!

    SLAVE 2 FREEZES

    SLAVE 1:   MORE!
                   MORE!
                   Bring him ..... **MORE!**

    SICKENING GOBBLING NOISES FROM THE STABLE

                             EXIT SLAVE 2

    SLAVE 1:   (Shouting) Keep kneeding!

ENTER. SLAVE 2: STAGGERING WITH A MASSIVE COWPAT
                        SLAVE 1 OFFERS PASSIVE ENCOURAGEMENT

      SLAVE 2:   (Throwing down pancake) **NO!**

SLAVE 1 IS DUMFOUNDED

SLAVE 2:   By Apollo ..... **NO!**
(Pause)
This **fffilth** here has proved too much for me.
I can't ssstand the ssstench a mmmmoment longer.

SLAVE 1 POINTS AT COWPAT DARES SLAVE 2

SLAVE 2:   Wwwhy don't I pppitch the entire dung-heap in?

SLAVE 1:   **Fine!** And throw yourself on top!

SLAVE 2 SIGHS LOUDLY, SHEEPISHLY RETRIEVES
COWPAT. THROWS IT FOR SLAVE 1 TO CATCH
SLAVE 1 DIVES FOR STABLE LIKE A FOOTBALLER

EXIT SLAVE 1.

ENTER. SLAVE 1: RACING BACK TO FETCH ANOTHER COWPAT

EXIT SLAVE 1.

SLAVE 2:   **(Aside)** Where can I buy a nose without holes?
(Muttering) Mmmashing dung .....
Mmmmashing ddung ..... to feed a beetle
(Pause)
What a dddemeaning loathsome mmmmiserable task.
(Sighing) A pig .... or dog will take a fair share of muck as it
falls: will take it as it comes.
But .... **This**!
(Pointing in the direction of the stable)
..... ccconceited brute!
(With nose high) Gives himself airs.
Won't touch a mmmouthful unless I've spent hours
rubbing, shaping and kneeding the dung!
You'd think it was Lllady Muck
not a fffilthy dung beetle. (Wiping hands on apron)

ENTER. SLAVE 1: CROSSING TO THE STABLE CARRYING A COWPAT

EXIT SLAVE 1.

LOUD GRUNTS FROM THE STABLE
SLAVE 2 TIPTOES OVER AND PEERS IN

SLAVE 2:   **Tuck in!**
Ddddon't stop.
I hope you gobble and guzzle 'till you burst.
(Recoiling in disgust)

Wretch
Throws himself on food like a heavyweight wrestler.
Sssstinking fffffoul .....

ENTER. SLAVE 1: WALKING OUT BACKWARDS FROM THE STABLE

SLAVE 2: .....gggluttonous vvvvoracious

SLAVE 1: This must be a terrible punishment brought down upon us by some god or other.

SLAVE 2: Who? Whhho'd associate with **him**?

SLAVE 1: Not Aphrodite I'd have thought!

SLAVE 2: (Sniggering) Nnnor the Graces.

SLAVE 1 TAKES SLAVE 2 BY THE SHOULDERS

SLAVE 1: Well! **Who?**

SLAVE 2: (Struggling to escape)
How should I know.
(Pause)
(Loud gasp)
Not .... Zzzzzeushimssself?

THEY SPIN AND STARE HEAVENWARDS IN AWE

SLAVE 1:} **ZEUS!**
SLAVE 2:} Zzzeus!

SLAVE 2: **(Aside)** But what's it all about?
(Pause)
Wwwhat's the significance of the beetle?

LOUD GRUNTS FROM THE STABLE

SLAVE 2: What can it mmmean?

SLAVE 1: I'm convinced that this whole thing is an allegory.....
(Pointing towards the stable)
Look at the shameless way it eats muck.
(Pausing thoughtfully)
Thrives on muck.
(Gasping with shock)
CLEON!

SLAVE 1: (Disparagingly) Ruthless dirty Demagogue.
Selfish dungbeetle of a leader
who managed to persuade the public
that he could lead the people of Athens to victory.

GRUNTS OF DELIGHT AT THE RECOGNITION

SLAVE 2: (Fawning subservient manner) III'lll ffffetch it a drink.

EXIT SLAVE 2.

SLAVE 1 SITS ON THE BALE OF HAY

SLAVE 1: **(Aside)** There's more to this .....
(Pause)
My Master ..... old Trygaeus is mad!
Not: **mad**, with old style war-mania.
Not: 'mad-about-war', the way people are.
No! His madness is quite novel.

ENTER. SLAVE 2: STAGGERING AWKWARDLY WITH OVERFULL PAIL

SLAVE 1: (Mimicking open mouthed vacant look)
All day long old Trygaeus gazes up at the sky .....
..... And **reviles Zeus!**
(Quavering voice)
'Oh! Zeus.'

SLAVE 2 PUTS DOWN THE PAIL, STANDS TO LISTEN

SLAVE 1: *(Quavering voice)*
'What do you hope to achieve?
Lay down your broom.
Don't sweep Greece bare!'

SLAVE 1 MOVES TOWARDS THE STABLE, LISTENS

SLAVE 1: *(Quavering voice)*
'Ah! Ah!'

SLAVE 2: Hear that?

SLAVE 1: *(Quavering voice)*
'Oh! Zeus.
What more do you want from our people?'

Must our cities be emptied because of the wars?
Will the lifeblood drain from our nation before you reconsider?'

SLAVE 2:	**(Aside)** Aaa............ sssample of the master's ravings
SLAVE 1:	**(Aside)** As I was saying .....
SLAVE 1:} **SLAVE 2:}**	... Mad .... quite .... mad. Mmmmadqquitemmmmad.
SLAVE 1:	**(Aside)** Possessed, mentally deranged.....
SLAVE 2:	**(Aside)** Ffffirst sign was when he ssstarted muttering to himself.
SLAVE 1:	*(Quavering voice)* 'Oh! (Pointing heavenwards) If only I could find a way to confront Zeus!'
SLAVE 2:	**(Aside)** Mmmaster had llightweight lladders made ......
SLAVE 1:	**(Aside)** My Master tried to scramble up to heaven ..... (Shaking head in disbelief) ... by ladder!
SLAVE 2:	**(Aside)** ......Mmmmaster ccame tumbling down ....And cccracked open his skull.

CRASHING AND BANGING FROM THE STABLE
BOTH SLAVES RESPOND APPREHENSIVELY

SLAVE 2:	**(Aside)** Then, Mmmaster crept off somewhere or other .... and brought home .... (Pointing towards the stable) **That abbommination!** A beetle... bbbigger than a man.

SLAVE 1 SHAKES HEAD SADLY, HANDS PAIL TO
SLAVE 2

SLAVE 2:	Mmmade me groom the freak of a jackass .... while he cccoaxed it .. (Shaking head forlornly) .. like a favourite ccolt.

SLAVE 1 EDGES CLOSE TO THE STABLE, LISTENS

SLAVE 1:	*(Quavering voice)* 'Wee Pegasus, my little flying thoroughbred,

your wings will sweep me heavenwards to Zeus.'

SLAVE 2:   IIIImagine! (Stiffling laughter)
             Old Trygaeus clinging to the back of a dung beetle
             (Setting down the pail) Ffflying up for a word with the Gods
             'for Greece'.

             THE SLAVES LAUGH TOGETHER

SLAVE 1:   Like something out of a tragedy.

SLAVE 2:   Mmmaster's not come out of the stable yet ....
             ....aaaand it's gone vvery quiet.

SLAVE 1:   I'll peep in and see what he's up to.

             SLAVE 1 CREEPS UP CLOSE
             SLAVE 2 SHADOWS, THEY TURN AND COLLIDE

SLAVE 1:}   .... **Oh!**
SLAVE 2:}   **Aaaaah!** ..... **Hhhelp!**
             (They follow an upward movement)
SLAVE 1:}   **Master!**
SLAVE 2:}   ..... **Mmmmmaster!**

SLAVE 1:   Master's astride the beetle ....and up they go!

SLAVE 2:   Mmmay the gods hhhhave mmercy upon us.
             Mmmaster's ffflying in the air.
SLAVE 1:   (Cutting in). Soaring to the gods
             ..... on a dungbeetle!

             THE SLAVES FALL TO THEIR KNEES STUPIFIED

PEACE CAN BE DIVIDED INTO 2 SHORT SCENES
FROM THE BEGINNING ......ENDING
'**Fine!** And throw yourself on top!' (Pages 45 - 48)
OR BEGINNING
'My Master ..... old Trygaues is mad!' (Pages 50-52)
THROUGH TO THE END

THE SIEVE AND OTHER SCENES
the first book
of original monologues
by Heather Stephens including
an adaptation of
THE LITTLE MATCH GIRL

THE SIEVE AND OTHER SCENES
ISBN 0 9522224 0 X
ISBN 0-88734-683-9

CABBAGE AND OTHER SCENES
the second book
of original monologues
by Heather Stephens including
an adaptation of
THE PIED PIPER OF HAMELIN

CABBAGE AND OTHER SCENES
ISBN 0 9522224 5 0
ISBN 0-88734-656-1

AN EXCELLENT INTRODUCTION TO SHAKESPEARE

Two one act plays by Paul Nimmo in
which famous speeches and scenes
from Shakespeare are acted out as
part of a comic story.

Suitable for performance by a large or
small cast aged 11 years upwards and
equally suitable for theatre group
performance to young people.

WILL SHAKESPEARE SAVE US! WILL SHAKESPEARE SAVE THE KIN
ISBN 0 9522224 1 8
ISBN 0-88734-658-8